2 0 JAN

2 5 FEB 2019   1 8 JUN 2019

WITHDRAWN

0 8 MAR 2019

2 8 NOV 2019

D0299848

This Orchard book

belongs to

....

Essex County Council

3013021091990 7

TEN LITTLE DINOSAURS

MIKE BROWNLOW SIMON RICKERTY

ORCHARD

Ten little dinosaurs, hatching from their eggs,
Blinking in the sunshine, stretching out their legs.
"Look! Our mummy's sleeping. Let's go and explore!"

Ten little dinosaurs all say . . .

"Roarrrrr!"

Ten little dinosaurs, walking in a line.

10

"Stomp!"

goes Diplodocus.

Now there are . . .

. . . nine.

9

Nine little dinosaurs think the world smells great!

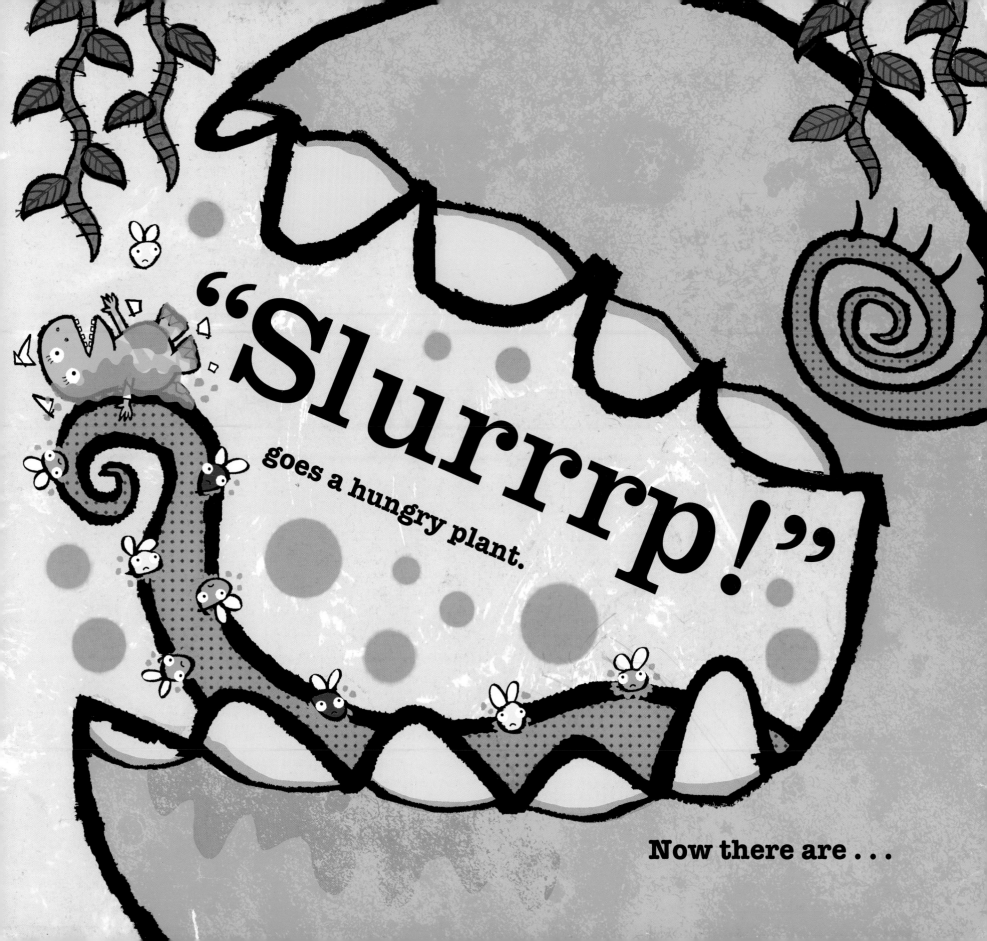

. . . eight.

Eight little dinosaurs
peep inside a cavern.

8

. . . seven.

Seven little dinosaurs
in a tricky fix.

7

"Caaaark!"

shrieks a pterosaur.

Now there are . . .

. . . six.

Six little dinosaurs

need to duck and dive.

6

"Sploosh!"

go the bubbling springs.

Now there are . . .

. . . five.

Five little dinosaurs hear an angry roar.

Charge!

goes Triceratops.

5

Now there are . . .

. . . **four.**

Four little dinosaurs, wobbling on a tree.

Snap!

goes the plesiosaur.

Now there are . . .

4

. . . three.

Three little dinosaurs,
trying to dodge the poo.

3

One little dinosaur. Has he met his doom?
What's that scary creature
stomping through the gloom?

It's not a raptor, not a T-Rex,
not a monster . . . PHEW!
It's Mum who's come to find him . . .
and all the others, too!

Safe at home with Mummy –

who could ask for more?

Ten little dinosaurs all say,

"Roarrrrrr!"

For Toby
M.B.

For Erin & Isla
S.R.

ORCHARD BOOKS
Carmelite House
50 Victoria Embankment
London EC4Y 0DZ

First published in 2015 by Orchard Books
This edition published in 2015

ISBN 978 1 40833 401 0

Text © Mike Brownlow 2015
Illustrations © Simon Rickerty 2015

The rights of Mike Brownlow to be identified as the author
and of Simon Rickerty to be identified as the illustrator of
this work have been asserted by them in accordance with
the Copyright, Designs and Patents Act, 1988.

A CIP catalogue record for this book is available from the British Library.

2 4 6 8 10 9 7 5 3 1

Printed in China

Orchard Books
An imprint of Hachette Children's Group
Part of The Watts Publishing Group Limited
An Hachette UK Company
www.hachette.co.uk